London Borough of Hounslow

...ole new world of animal...

The creature nestled in Charlie's arms. Its fur was as soft as the fluff on a newborn chick and the stripe on its back seemed to glisten like a river of silver in the soft evening light.

"That's what I'm going to call you," Charlie decided. "Silver. That's your name."

Look out for:

The Friendly Firecat

The Helpful Hootpuff

COSMIC CREATURES

A whole new world of animal rescue!

The Runaway Rumblebear

ILLUSTRATED BY SOPHY WILLIAMS

TOM HUDDLESTON

nosy crow

First published in the UK in 2022 by Nosy Crow Ltd
The Crow's Nest, 14 Baden Place
Crosby Row, London, SE1 1YW, UK

Nosy Crow Eireann Ltd
44 Orchard Grove, Kenmare,
Co Kerry, V93 FY22, Ireland

www.nosycrow.com

ISBN: 978 1 83994 127 6

Nosy Crow and associated logos are trademarks and/or
registered trademarks of Nosy Crow Ltd

Text copyright © Tom Huddleston, 2022
Illustrations © Sophy Williams, 2022

A CIP catalogue record for this book will be available from the British Library

Printed and bound in Great Britain by Clays Ltd, Elcograf S.p.A.

Papers used by Nosy Crow are made from wood grown in sustainable forests.

1 3 5 7 9 10 8 6 4 2

Chapter One
The Vanishing Apples

Charlie looked up at the tall white tree. Its top branches were bowed down with sparkly blue shimmer-apples.

"Come on, Random," she called out. "Let's get picking!"

But Random the robot wasn't paying any attention.

His ball-shaped body floated above the ground. His metal arms were stretched out wide and his silver eyes flashed with

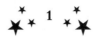

concentration.

His hands twirled

as five shimmer-apples bounced

between them.

Charlie grinned. "That's very clever," she said. "But we're here to pick the apples, Random. Not juggle them."

Random tried to stop juggling, but the apples were flying too fast for him. His arms began to whir madly and his body spun like a top.

Finally the apples went flying and splatted to the ground.

Random came to a stop, floating upside down. "Oops," he said.

Charlie laughed. Random was her best friend but sometimes his wiring could be a little wonky. "You know you shouldn't play with your food!" she said.

The robot righted himself and looked at Charlie sheepishly. "They'd already fallen from the tree," he said. "And I really thought I could do it."

"I know," Charlie said kindly. "But we can't afford to waste anything since those crops went missing."

Three times in the past week, the contents of an entire storage barn had vanished. Not a berry, a bean, or an ear of corn had been left behind.

A short time ago, it wouldn't have mattered. The people of First Landing had brought their Make-o-Mat machine with them from Earth. It could create any kind of food they wanted, from comet-candy to Martian meatballs.

But the machine had broken down months ago, and the next repair ship wouldn't arrive on Vela for a long time. So for now they had to rely on whatever food they could forage or grow themselves in the soil of their new home.

Luckily there were lots of plants on Vela that were good for humans to eat. It was one of the reasons they'd chosen this planet in the first place. Also, they had special super-grow powder to make sure the plants grew faster. But it was still hard work making sure everyone was fed.

And now someone – or some*thing* – was stealing their crops!

There was a sudden loud rustle and Random whirled around. Charlie followed his gaze and – just for a moment – she thought she saw the grass of the orchard waving, as though something had just vanished into the undergrowth.

"Did you hear that?" she asked Random.

The robot rocked back and forth – it was his way of nodding.

"It could have been the wind," he said.

Charlie frowned. She could feel a breeze blowing, though it didn't seem strong enough to have made such a loud and surprising noise.

She kept listening, but the noise didn't come again. She grabbed her basket and shrugged. "Whatever it was, it's gone now," she said. "So we'd better get picking."

Right at the very top of the tree she could see a cluster of shimmer-apples, sparkling in the sun. "Can you lift me up?" she asked. "I'll pick the trickiest ones first."

"Good idea," Random said, and he
began to make a deep humming noise.

The robot was surrounded by a force
field that kept him floating above the
ground. If he made it larger, he could
wrap it around Charlie too.

She felt a familiar tingling as her feet

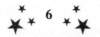

left the ground.
She floated
upwards until she
was level with the
top of the tree.
From there, she
could see right across
the colourful jumble of roofs
that made up the town of First
Landing. She could see silver hover-
carts gliding through the winding
streets, and if she listened carefully, she
could even hear the chatter of voices
from the main square.

Beyond the town she could make
out the huge starship that had brought
them to Vela. Its silver-black dome
rose above all the other buildings, and
its giant rockets stood out against the
violet sky. A crescent moon peeked
above it like an emerald jewel.

Cosmic Creatures

This is the most beautiful planet in the universe, she thought happily. *I'm so lucky to live here.*

Charlie had arrived on Vela two years ago, along with her parents and her little brother and three hundred other people. They were the first humans to settle on this faraway planet, with its twin suns and five moons. Their mission was to study the local plants and animals, without interfering with the planet's delicate natural balance.

Her memories of the long journey to get here had already started to fade. So had her memories of Earth, the planet where she'd been born ten years ago. She wondered if she would ever go back there again.

Charlie plucked a handful of shimmer-apples, placing them gently in her basket. They smelled so delicious that she could hardly resist taking a bite. But she knew the rules: every scrap of food had to be shared equally among the settlers. It wouldn't be fair for her to tuck in.

She saw a blue sparkle through the branches and reached her hand out for the apple. The leaves brushed her face as she stretched further, as far as she could, held up by Random's powerful force field.

Suddenly she felt something. But it wasn't an apple.

It was warm.

And furry.

And moving.

Charlie yanked her hand back in surprise as the branches parted and two green eyes stared at her. Then the leaves swung back and the eyes disappeared. The tree shook, branches stirring as something moved around inside.

"Random!" she called. "Bring me down!"

COSMIC CREATURES

Charlie floated down, landing neatly on the orchard floor. Above her the tree was rustling wildly. Then a dark shape jumped down from a low branch and darted away through the long grass.

The orchard was surrounded by a wall

of bushes with green, russet and orange leaves. This was the edge of Akira Forest, the immense woodland that covered the hills beyond First Landing. The colourful bushes stirred for a few moments, then silence fell.

"What was that?" Charlie whispered to Random. "Did you get a good look at it?"

"It was too quick," the robot said. "But I think I know why it was here."

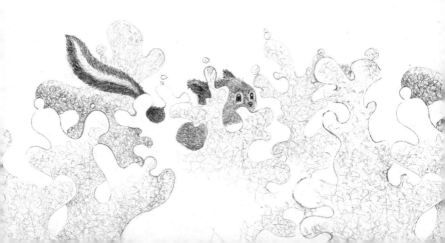

He pointed up into the branches.
Horrified, Charlie saw what he meant.

The white leaves still fluttered in the
breeze, but the blue shimmer-apples
that had hung there were gone.

Charlie looked around the orchard
and her heart sank. Each tree had
been stripped bare. Every apple in the
orchard had been taken. And she and
Random had been so distracted, they
hadn't even noticed.

"We have to follow it, whatever
it was," Charlie said firmly, starting
towards the forest. "We can't just let it
steal all our apples."

"B-but –" Random protested, floating
after her. "What if it's dangerous? It
might be a terrible beast!"

Charlie did not slow down. "We've
been on this planet nearly two years
and we haven't met any dangerous

creatures yet," she said. "And anyway, if it was a terrible beast, it would have tried to eat us, not the apples. So let's go!"

Chapter Two
Silver

They stopped at the edge of the forest and Charlie's mouth dropped open.

Ahead of them, a wall of brightly coloured bushes marked the boundary of the orchard. But many of the bushes lay in tatters. Charlie saw broken branches and scattered leaves, and the forest floor was all torn up as though a herd of wild oxpigs had come charging through.

"This isn't the work of a single creature,"

Random said, scanning the destruction with his bright electronic eyes. "There must be a pack."

"Come on, then," Charlie said. "Let's follow them while the trail's still fresh."

Random looked uncertainly between the trees. "Very well, but let me g-go f-first," he said nervously. "Then if anything happens I can p-protect you."

Charlie hid her smile. Random wasn't a soldier or a security droid – in fact he'd been designed as a constructor robot, part of the mechanical crew that had been sent to Vela to build a town for the human settlers. But there had been an accident. A building had collapsed and Random had been trapped inside.

He'd been lying on a scrapheap when Charlie found him. He had one arm missing and his memory banks were badly rusted. Her mother had helped

Charlie to
repair him
and he'd
lived with
them
ever since.
His circuits had
never completely
recovered, but Charlie
thought he was
the best robot in the
universe. And the best
friend, too.

They kept quiet as they moved deeper
into Akira Forest.

Huge grey-green trunks towered over
them. Red, orange and purple leaves
littered the mossy ground. Sunlight fell in
long shafts and birdsong echoed from the
high branches like music. She heard soft
squeaks and snuffles and saw a family of

green-tailed furbits scurrying off into their holes.

Charlie had been in the forest before. It was right on her doorstep, after all. But she'd never had time to really explore it. Between her chores at home, her lessons at school and helping with the harvest, she always seemed to be too busy.

Now she looked around in wonder, as the trees rose taller and the silence grew deeper. She was glad of Random at her side, his force field humming as he floated along.

There was a noise ahead of them. It was so loud and so sudden that Random instinctively extended his force field, wrapping it around Charlie to protect her.

Clutching Random, Charlie peered nervously into the undergrowth. The noise had been like a rumble of thunder, or like the lions she'd seen in old clips from

Earth. A roar…

She remembered what Random had said about a terrible beast, and shivered. What if there was something out there, something the settlers hadn't spotted before? She bit her lip. She had to be brave.

The roar erupted again and Random let out a fearful beep. The earth shook with the force of the sound. Charlie felt her knees tremble.

Then the leaves parted and something came towards them, casting a long shadow. The sunlight slanted through the trees and a furry shape was revealed.

The creature looked at Charlie with large green eyes, just the same colour as the ones she'd encountered up in the apple tree. Its fur was all standing up, like it was trying to make itself look bigger and more fierce. It didn't really work.

"Oh," Charlie said in surprise. "It's a lot smaller than I was expecting."

The creature was about the size of a puppy. It only came up to Charlie's knees, even with all its fur on end. It had a bushy tail that whisked from side to side, and was covered in bright-red fur with a shiny silver stripe along the back. Its big eyes looked up at her hopefully.

Charlie had never seen or heard of any animal like it before, not in all her time on Vela. This was a whole new species – and she was the first to meet it.

She crouched, reaching out her hand. "Hello, little friend," she said. "Were you the one making all that—"

The creature bounded forward, jumping into Charlie's arms. Then it roared again, a deafening bellow that almost made her topple over backwards.

Random spun upside down in surprise.

Then the creature shut its mouth and the sound stopped abruptly.

"How can such a little thing make such a big noise?" Charlie asked as the roar echoed away through the forest.

"I've no idea," Random admitted. "I'm just glad it's not a terrible beast."

The creature nuzzled against Charlie's

arm and she stroked its silver-striped fur. Then she noticed something. Around its mouth were little flecks of sparkly blue peel.

"Well, he's definitely one of the shimmer-apple thieves," she said. "Hang on, maybe he and his pack took our other stores too! But where are the rest of them?"

"The trail continues that way." Random pointed ahead.

"Oh, he must've got left behind!" Charlie realised, scratching the creature on its furry head. "Maybe that's why he was roaring like that. Poor thing, I think he's only a baby. We have to try to get him back to his family."

Random looked around doubtfully. "I don't think we should go any further tonight. The second sun's setting, it'll be dark soon."

"But we can't just leave him here," Charlie protested. "Not all alone in the forest. Not at night!"

The creature gave a rumble of agreement, but to Charlie's relief he didn't let out another of those earth-shaking roars. She came to a decision, clasped him carefully around the belly and lifted him as she got to her feet.

"We'll take him home with us," she told Random. "Then in the morning we can follow the trail and find the rest of his pack."

"The other settlers might not like it," Random warned. "Especially if they find out your new friend is part of the pack who have been stealing their stores."

"Then he'll have to be our secret," Charlie whispered. "It's just for one night, after all. We'll come back first thing tomorrow and no one will have to know."

Random looked uncertain. "I don't know if it's such a good idea."

Charlie tipped her head, treating the robot to one of her most winning smiles. The creature joined in, batting its long eyelashes and letting out a purr so soft and hopeful that Charlie had to fight back a laugh.

"Oh, all right," said Random with an electronic sigh. "What's the worst that could happen?"

The creature nestled in Charlie's arms. Its fur was as soft as the fluff on a newborn chick and the stripe on its back seemed to glisten like a river of silver in the soft evening light.

"That's what I'm going to call you," Charlie decided. "Silver. That's your name."

Silver curled himself up, letting out a
deep, contented rumble. It was almost
as if the little creature understood what
she was saying.

"But when we get back to town you'll

have to stay out of sight," she told him.
"And try to keep quiet, OK? No more
big roars!"

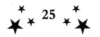

Chapter Three
The Captain's Plan

The second sun was just touching the horizon as Charlie stepped from the cover of the trees. The evening light was a rich golden colour and the air was full of darting insects and dancing specks of pollen.

Charlie had hoped to sneak through the orchard without being seen. But before she'd taken three steps out of the forest, she heard a shout and looked up.

Her mother, Shona, was standing among the apple trees with two of her fellow settlers. All of them were looking in dismay at the bare branches. Shona beckoned urgently and Charlie turned to Random.

"You have to hide Silver!" she said. The little creature's ears pricked up at the mention of his name. "We can't let Mum or the others see him."

"Hide him where?" Random asked. Then he realised what she meant. "Oh no! Out of the question!"

"Come on," Charlie pleaded. "Silver will be good. Won't you?"

Silver purred and growled and seemed to be on the verge of letting out one of his enormous roars when Random relented. There was a hum of motors and a hatch on the side of the robot's body slid open.

"Let's hope he stays quiet," Random

said as Charlie tucked Silver inside the secret compartment. "One of those loud roars and I might fall apart!"

The hatch slid shut as they started across the meadow towards Charlie's mum and her companions. Shona's red hair was tied back in a bun and her hands were filthy with engine grease.

She was wearing a flowery sundress that Charlie and Random had helped her to stitch out of an old bed sheet.

That was another unexpected result of the Make-o-Mat machine being broken. The people of Vela couldn't just order all the clothes they needed any more. They had been forced to make their own.

The others were dressed in an assortment of handmade robes stitched out of curtains, tablecloths and even old food sacks. A red-faced man had "Real Earth Beetroot" printed in big letters across his chest, and Charlie had to try hard not to giggle.

COSMIC CREATURES

"You and Random were on apple-picking duty today, weren't you, Charlie?" Shona asked as they came closer. "Did you see what happened?"

"We saw … something," Charlie said carefully. Random was right – the people of First Landing wouldn't be happy to find out Silver and his pack had stolen their apples. "The creatures ran off before we could get a good look."

"Creatures?" Shona asked. "So there was more

than one?"

Charlie nodded. "We tried to follow their trail but it started to get dark," she said. "We didn't want you to worry, so we decided to come back."

Shona's eyes narrowed. "You're not usually so cautious. Why didn't you call me on your mini-com? We could've searched the woods together."

Charlie felt her face heat up. She opened her mouth, but before she could speak, she was interrupted by a loud, high-pitched voice.

"What is the meaning of this? What has happened to all our lovely apples?"

She turned to see a short man with a large moustache striding between the trees. Akira Robertson had been Captain on the spaceship that had brought them to Vela, and he was still officially in charge. He was a fidgety, excitable man

who loved the sound of his own voice —
especially when it was shouting. And he
still insisted on being called Captain, even
though the ship hadn't flown in years.

"Who did this?" he bellowed, pointing a
trembling finger up into the branches. "I
want them found! I want them caught! I
want them brought to justice!"

"We were just trying to get to the
bottom of it, Captain," Shona told him.
"My daughter believes the shimmer-
apples were taken by some kind of
creatures."

The captain's eyebrows shot up like
leaping caterpillars. "Creatures?" he said
in horror. "In *my forest*?"

In a way, it was true. Akira Forest had
been named after the captain. In fact,
everything in and around First Landing
was named after one of the settlers.
There was a Shona Beach on the other

side of town, and a little stream called Charlie's Brook ran past the farmhouse where they lived.

But it didn't really mean that the captain owned the forest. He just acted like it was his property.

"We must post guards!" he said, twisting his moustache restlessly with his fingers. "I want security droids all around the town. And we need to put up a fence. A high one, with an electric charge. That'll show them."

The other settlers nodded in agreement, but Shona frowned doubtfully.

"We didn't travel hundreds of light years just to live behind a fence," she said. "We're here to explore this planet, to learn and study. Not to shut ourselves in. Anyway, Charlie knows which way the creatures went. She tried to follow them, but unfortunately they got away."

Cosmic Creatures

Captain Robertson turned on Charlie, bending down until his face was just centimetres from hers. "You saw them?" he demanded. "How big were they? How many were there? Did they look fierce?"

Charlie gulped. She looked at Random, who floated silently beside her. She could hear a faint rumbling

from inside his storage compartment and quickly started speaking to cover it up.

"The one we saw was quite small," she said truthfully. "But they left a big trail behind them."

The captain gave a cunning smile and clasped his hands together.

"Good," he said. "Very good. Tomorrow I want you to show me where to find this trail. We'll track these beasts down and find out exactly what they're up to.

"You can come along with us," he said, pointing to Shona. "Carl, Padma, you too." He pointed to the other two townsfolk. "Just in case they prove dangerous."

"But I was going to take my boys to the beach…" the red-faced man protested.

But the captain waved a hand. "This is more important," he barked. "I won't have thieves lurking about in my forest. I just won't have it!"

There was a sudden loud rumbling sound, muffled and echoing but definitely close by. Everyone turned in surprise and their eyes finally settled on Random.

The robot's body vibrated as the roar faded away. He looked at Charlie, who shrugged helplessly. Random raised his hands.

"I'm very sorry everyone," he said. "It must be something I ate."

Chapter Four
The Rockfruit

"That was close," Charlie whispered as they hurried home across the fields.

In the streets of First Landing the electric lamps were starting to buzz and flicker. Overhead the third moon was rising, pearly-white in the purple sky.

"I didn't know what to say," Random admitted. "Your mother gave me quite a suspicious look."

"Well, she probably remembered that

robots don't eat!" Charlie laughed.

She could see the farmhouse up ahead. The windows shone welcomingly in the dusk. Like every other building in First Landing, it was made from grey slabs of metal and plastic. But Charlie's family had done all they could to make it feel like home.

There were bright flowerbeds in the front garden and a shingle path leading from the wooden gate. A solar-powered lantern blazed above the front door.

"I'll finish my chores as quick as I can," Charlie told Random. "Take Silver upstairs and try to keep him out of sight. I'll be right back."

She grabbed a plastic bucket from the porch then she crossed the courtyard to the cattle shed. Luna the mooncalf stood sleepily in her stall, snuffling softly and glowing with a pale, silky light.

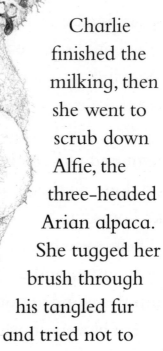

Charlie finished the milking, then she went to scrub down Alfie, the three-headed Arian alpaca. She tugged her brush through his tangled fur and tried not to get licked too many times. Three heads meant three tongues, after all.

Her last job was to feed the pigs, a pair of bristly Earth hogs called Grunt and Grumble. Her parents had chosen the animals on their farm with the utmost care, taking into account how well they'd adapt to life on Vela. Some were native to Earth, while other species came from far-off planets – places Charlie could only imagine.

When they saw Charlie coming, the pigs lumbered towards her. As she entered the sty, they lowered their heads and butted her ankles in a friendly but rather unhelpful manner. Charlie struggled to keep her balance as she tipped a pail of slops into their trough.

Then a thought struck her and she picked up a handful of roots and vegetable scraps, stuffing them into her pocket. They'd stink, but she could always wash her jacket later.

As she hurried back home she could see her dad in the top field, checking his new crop of night-wheat by the light of the moons. Kwame lifted a hand, waving at her across the shimmering meadow.

Charlie waved back, then she slipped through the farmhouse door. She wanted to get upstairs to her room without being spotted.

"What are you doing?" a voice demanded, and her heart sank.

Her brother Maki was watching her from a stool by the kitchen counter. He had his sketch pad and a pack of colouring pencils out.

"Why are you sneaking around?" he

said. Maki had just turned seven, and he always seemed to find an excuse to get in Charlie's way.

"I wasn't sneaking," she said. "I was just walking normally."

"Then why did you close the front door so carefully?" Maki asked, slipping down from his stool and coming towards her. "And why did you tiptoe? And why are

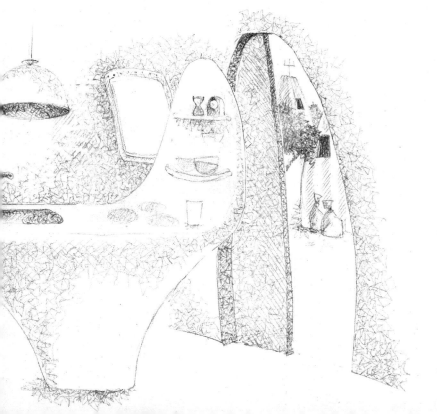

you blushing?"

Charlie gave a sigh of frustration. "I'm blushing because I've been lifting heavy slop buckets. And I was tiptoeing because I didn't want you to know I was home and come and bother me. Exactly like you're doing now."

Maki frowned. "I don't believe you. I think you've got a secret you're not telling me. Is it food? Is it sweets?"

He leaned closer and sniffed, then he wrinkled his nose. "Ew. You smell awful. What's in your pocket? A load of rubbish?"

"Yes," she told him. "And if you're not careful I'll put it in your supper!"

She turned and marched up the stairs, leaving him standing at the bottom.

"But why have you got pockets full of rubbish?" he shouted after her. "What do you want it for? Charlie!"

She shut her bedroom door and took a deep breath. Then she heard a rumbling noise and spun round.

Silver was sitting on her worktable. His bushy red tail whisked happily when he saw Charlie, and the silver stripe gleamed in the lamplight.

She gave her new friend a tickle under the chin and he growled a welcome. Then he rolled on his back like he wanted her to stroke his tummy.

Charlie ruffled his soft fur. "That's a good boy," she said, and Silver showed his teeth. Again she got the feeling that the little creature understood everything she said.

Charlie gave such a good tummy rub that Silver threw back his head and let out his loudest roar yet. It was so deafening that it made the table shake.

Charlie pulled her hand back. "No,

Silver!" she hissed. "You have to stay quiet."

"He seems to make the loudest noises when he's happy," Random observed, floating towards the desk. "Or perhaps when he's hungry."

"Oh, that reminds me," Charlie said. She emptied her pocket, pulling out smelly brown apple cores and scraps of dug-up roots. Silver looked at the slops doubtfully, then he spotted something and his eyes went wide.

He sprang forward, grabbing a small black object in his front paws. He stuffed it into his mouth and chomped noisily. Then he rifled through the scraps with his paws.

He found another of the shiny black fruits and devoured it. Afterwards, he looked up at Charlie and gave a loud, delighted gurgle.

"You liked that, didn't you?" Charlie asked, picking out more of the strange black objects. "I wonder what it is? Maybe it—"

"Supper time!" boomed a voice from right outside the room.

Charlie jumped, gathering Silver up quickly. She hid him behind her back just as her father put his head through the doorway.

"Time for you to set the table," Kwame grinned. "Or I'll tickle you with these."

He held up his hands. They were covered with soil, all the way up to the elbows. Charlie jumped back with a squeal.

"I was just coming," she said. "Wasn't I, Random?"

The robot nodded. "Oh, yes. Absolutely. Right on the verge."

Kwame looked down at the table, spotting the little pile of black fruits.

"What are you doing with those?" he asked, wrinkling his nose. "Don't try to eat one, you'll break your teeth."

"I'm not," Charlie said. She could feel

Silver wriggling and tickling in her hands.
It was almost impossible not to laugh.
"They're, um … for a school project. We
were asked to find native plants to, er,
study."

Kwame nodded. "You know, there used
to be a big grove of them, right where
the orchard is now," he said. "But when
our beloved captain found out they were
inedible, he ordered them cut down and

planted shimmer-apples instead. There was a bit of a row about it, actually. We're not supposed to do things like that."

"So where did these ones come from?" Charlie asked. "How did they end up in Grunt and Grumble's food?"

"There are still a few trees down at the bottom of the valley," Kwame explained. "The pigs were snuffling around one day and they ate those things whole. They seemed to like them, so whenever I'm down there I pick up a handful. Now come on, Mum didn't cook you a nice dinner so it could sit around getting cold."

"I'll be right there, promise," Charlie said, fighting back a grin as Silver tickled her palms. "Just give me one minute to get, um, cleaned up."

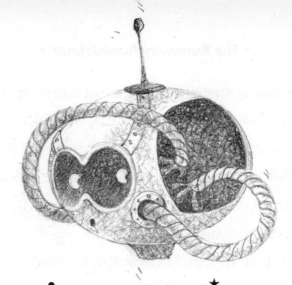

Chapter Five
Silver's Escape

After dinner Charlie returned to her room to find Silver curled up inside Random's secret compartment, snoring softly. She got into bed as quietly as she could, so as not to disturb him.

Random didn't sleep, of course. He just plugged himself into the power socket and closed his systems down. As always, he spent the night floating next to Charlie's bed, and the hum of his circuits was the last thing she heard as she drifted off to sleep.

She was woken the next morning by a knock on her bedroom door. She sat up in surprise, blinking and bleary-eyed.

"I hope you're getting up," her mother called. "I've had a message to meet Captain Robertson in the town square in ten minutes. He's desperate to go and track down these thieves of yours."

The door started to open. Charlie suddenly realised that she needed to get Silver out of sight.

Random was still floating beside the bed. His golden eyes flickered as his artificial brain came back to life.

His storage hatch stood open. But the space inside was empty.

Charlie pointed in horror. "Random, look!" she whispered. "He's gone!"

The robot looked down in surprise,

feeling around inside the compartment. But before he could speak, Shona entered the room.

"Charlie, you're not even dressed!" she said, clapping her hands. "Come on, quickly now."

Charlie sat bolt upright. She needed to think fast.

"You'll have to, umm…" she started. "You'll have to go without me. There's something I really need to do. I'll be right behind you!"

Shona looked at her daughter doubtfully. "Well, all right," she said. "I'll tell the captain you're on your way. But you know how he hates to be kept waiting."

She puffed out her cheeks and scowled, fiddling with a pretend moustache.

Charlie giggled. "I'll be really quick. I promise!"

Shona left the room. Moments later Charlie heard the front door close.

Charlie scrambled to pull on her trousers while Random scanned the room with his sensors. "I'm afraid there is no sign of our little friend," he said.

"Well, keep looking!" said Charlie. "Let's hope we can find him before he tries to eat everything."

Just as she spoke there was a crash downstairs then a loud rumble. Charlie knew right away what was happening.

"The kitchen!" she said. "Come on!"

They hurtled down the stairs and along the corridor. Charlie grabbed the kitchen door and threw it open. The sight that greeted her was worse than she could have imagined.

The floor was strewn with food. There was cereal and sugar and crusts of bread. There were pools of milk and piles of squashed, half-eaten fruit. Bowls and containers were scattered on the counter. Her dad's favourite coffee mug lay in three pieces on the floor.

Charlie stood frozen in the doorway. Random bobbed at her side.

"I think he went that way," he said, and pointed to the back door. It stood half-open.

Charlie started towards it. "We have to go after him."

But before she could reach it, a voice

boomed behind her.

"What in the million moons of Macondo is going on here?"

Charlie spun round. Her father stood open-mouthed, looking at the mess.

Maki pushed past, his eyes wide with amazement.

"Wow, Charlie," he said. "What did you eat for breakfast? Everything in the *world*?"

Charlie spluttered. "The thieves!" she managed. "It must have been the thieves." It was sort of true, she told herself. Silver was one of them, after all.

Kwame nodded. "Of course. The same ones who took the apples," he said. "But I didn't think they'd be bold enough to invade someone's kitchen."

He grabbed his coat from the back of a chair. "Come on, let's join your mum and tell Captain Robertson."

Charlie struggled to think of an excuse not to go. She really wanted to stay and hunt for Silver. But the little creature could be anywhere, and her father looked determined.

"All right," she said, pulling on her boots and her ultra-seal jacket.

"I'll come too!" Maki said excitedly. "I can tell everyone what a mess there was!"

The twin suns of Vela were blazing

overhead as they set out. Kwame strode on ahead, with Maki hurrying at his heels. Charlie fell back, talking quietly to Random.

"Keep your eyes peeled for Silver," she said. "Hopefully he hasn't had time to cause any more trouble or raid any more kitchens."

"Perhaps he has returned to the forest to find his pack," Random said. "That might be for the best."

Charlie frowned. "I suppose so. But what if he can't find them and gets lost again? He's only small, after all. Oh, Random, I hope he's OK!"

The streets of First Landing were bustling with people and vehicles. Everyone was dressed in homemade costumes stitched from curtains and pillows. They were so colourful that the main street looked like a field of flowers.

Cosmic Creatures

A pair of five-metre-tall lifter droids thumped along the street, casting their shadows over Random. He floated closer to Charlie, looking up nervously.

A hover-cart glided past, piled high with machine parts. It was driven by a boy Charlie knew from school. He waved and she forced a smile, trying not to worry about Silver.

In the town square a group of settlers were hard at work sorting baskets of vegetables and grain. They were dividing up that week's rations so they could be shared equally among the people.

Nearby, Captain Robertson stood with Shona and the other settlers from yesterday, Padma and Carl. Kwame approached them, and Charlie heard Maki telling everyone what had happened in their kitchen.

"Those monsters!" the captain bellowed.

"To attack a person in their home!"
Kwame frowned. "I wouldn't say they attacked anyone, exactly…"

"Oh, they most certainly did!" the captain told him, twisting his moustache excitedly. "And they must be stopped! They must be tracked down in their lair, and rooted out! And I, Captain Akira Robertson, intend to do it!"

He turned to Charlie. "Are you ready, young lady? Are you ready to set out on this vital quest to save your town from these beasts?"

Charlie didn't know what to say. "Um, I suppose so," she managed.

The captain beamed. "Very good. This will be a great day, mark my words. A proud moment in the history of First Landing. I may even write a song about it."

Charlie groaned inwardly. The captain's songs were famously terrible, and they all went on for hours.

"I'll call it the Ballad of Akira Forest,"

he said. "A heroic tale of bravery and
great deeds and—"

There was a sudden cry from across the
square.

Charlie turned. At first she couldn't
tell what was happening. The townsfolk
who'd been sorting the food were all
jumping to their feet.

She saw a basket go flying into the air,
then another.

Then there was a familiar deafening
roar, and panic broke out.

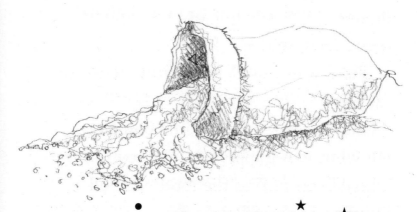

Chapter Six
The Captain's Rucksack

People began to run back and forth, waving their arms and shrieking.

Charlie grabbed Random. "It must be Silver," she cried. "Come on, we have to save him!"

The roar erupted again, echoing from the buildings on every side. Captain Robertson charged towards the sound.

Shona and Kwame were close behind him.

"Catch the thief!" the captain yelled. "Grab it! Stop it! Don't let it get away!"

Baskets lay scattered all across the cobbles. Fruit and grain were flying everywhere. People stampeded wildly, hunting for the culprit.

Shona stood in the centre of it all, holding up her hands and calling for calm.

"We need this food!" she was shouting. "Everyone, settle down!"

The captain ran back and forth, tipping over barrels and looking under crates. "Come out, fiend!" he barked. "Come out and face justice!"

He twisted round, surveying the square. And as he did so, Charlie saw that he was wearing a red rucksack with a silver stripe. Had he been wearing it before?

Then she realised and her mouth dropped open.

"Look!" she whispered to Random. "There he is!"

Silver clung to the captain's back with his front claws. The captain marched up and down. He barked orders and gestured with both hands. He hadn't noticed the little creature and neither had anyone else. But it wouldn't be long before they did.

Charlie ran towards the captain. She had to tread carefully on the food-splattered stones. Silver saw her and opened his mouth happily.

Charlie shook her head and held out her arms. Silver jumped into them, purring and nuzzling against her cheek.

The captain turned quickly. Charlie stuffed Silver inside her jacket as fast as she could and tugged up the zip.

Captain Robertson's eyes narrowed. "What was that?" he hissed. He reached with both arms to try to touch his back. "I'm sure I felt something."

"It was a twinklcfly," Charlie said. "Big one, too. Look, there it goes!"

She pointed into the sky, and as the captain looked up she stuffed Silver down further. She tried not to giggle as his soft fur tickled her belly.

"I don't see it," the captain said. "But I suppose it must have been there."

The commotion in the square had started to calm down. The people were beginning to gather up all the spilled food.

The captain frowned and stamped his foot, crushing a tomato. "We must not let this distract us from our mission," he said. "No doubt that is what the fiend and its kind want."

"So you're still going after them?" Charlie asked.

"Of course!" the captain replied. "And you're coming with me."

Charlie felt her heart pound. What was she going to do?

She couldn't go with the captain, not with Silver under her jacket. Even hiding him in Random's storage compartment wouldn't be enough. Sooner or later, someone would hear him.

She had to get him back to his pack before he caused any more mischief.

Suddenly she felt someone tugging on

her hand. Maki was staring at her jacket, which was bulging and shifting in a most unusual manner.

"What's that?" he asked loudly. "Charlie, what's—"

"Shhh!" she said. And suddenly a plan came to her.

She glanced back at the captain. To her relief, he was distracted. He was talking to her parents, pointing an angry finger towards the forest.

Charlie pulled her little brother aside. Slowly she tugged down her zip.

Silver peeked out. His green eyes glinted in the shadows.

Maki's jaw dropped open. "But that's… But you…"

"His name's Silver," Charlie whispered. "He's the one who wrecked our kitchen."

"But what is he?" Maki asked. "I've never seen anything like him before. Even

in a book!"

Charlie shrugged. "I suppose his species doesn't have a name yet," she said. "But listen, if you help me, I'll let you make one up."

Maki beamed, and Silver let out a happy growl.

"Charlie, it sounds like your belly's

rumbling," Maki chuckled. "I know – that's what we should call them. Rumblebears!"

Charlie smiled. "I like it. Hello, little rumblebear." She cuddled Silver through her jacket.

Silver made another deep, joyful noise, and it was settled.

Under her breath, Charlie told her little brother exactly what she wanted him to do. "We'll stay in touch with our mini-coms," she went on, and held up the little device that she kept in her pocket.

Maki nodded, grinning with excitement.

When she was sure no one was watching, Charlie slid Silver inside Random's storage compartment. Then she walked over to her parents, groaning and holding her belly.

"I feel really sick," she said. "I think it must be something I ate."

Shona placed a hand on Charlie's forehead, looking down at her with concern. Then she leaned close, whispering in her ear.

"I know something's going on," she said. "What are you up to?"

Charlie blushed. "I'll tell you later," she whispered back. "I promise."

Shona nodded. "All right. I trust you."

Then she turned back to Captain Robertson, shaking her head sadly.

"I'm afraid Charlie won't be able join us today," she said. "I think she's coming down with something."

The captain opened his mouth to protest, but Charlie spoke first.

"It's not hard to find the trail," she said. "I'll describe exactly where to look. You really can't miss it."

Then she groaned and clutched her stomach again.

Chapter Seven
In a Tangle

Charlie and Random hurried back to the farmhouse, where she packed her rucksack with a bottle of water and two shimmer-apples for the journey.

"There's just one more thing I want to get," she said as they crossed the farm courtyard. She walked over to the pig pen, where Grunt and Grumble were standing with their front trotters on the fence. There was a heap of waste food nearby –

rotting vegetables and scraps of fruit.

Charlie took a bag from her pocket and carefully picked out the rockfruits. She put most of them in the bag, handing a couple to Silver to keep him happy. He wolfed them down, the cracking and chomping loud beneath Charlie's jacket.

"Silver's crazy about these rockfruits," she said, pocketing the bag. "So I bet the rest of his pack will be, too."

"Good thinking," Random agreed. He looked up at the great forest covering the slopes above them. A stiff wind blew and the colourful trees creaked and shifted. "Now all we have to do is find them before the captain does."

Even after a night and a morning, the broad trail left by Silver's pack was easy to find and to follow. Charlie put Silver down and the little

creature raced excitedly through the undergrowth, sniffing and purring and leading the way.

Cosmic Creatures

The sunlight slanted in multicoloured shafts between the leaves. All around them Charlie could hear the hum and whine of strange insects and the trilling of distant birds. Once she saw a flock of sparrowkeets up near the forest canopy, a spiral of bright-blue wings, swooping and diving in the light.

She could also hear the search party up ahead. Captain Robertson and his fellow settlers went crashing through the undergrowth like a herd of giraffaloes.

"Maki, we're catching up," Charlie whispered into her mini-com. "I need a distraction so we can sneak past!"

"I'll do my best," her brother answered. "I already told everyone I saw something moving in the trees. That slowed them down while Dad went to look. Then I fell into a tangleberry bush and pretended I couldn't get out again."

Charlie grinned. "That sounds funny."

"But the Captain's really on a mission," Maki went on. "He keeps telling everyone to walk faster!"

"It's because he thinks it's his forest," Charlie whispered back. "And he thinks Silver and his pack have invaded it. Never mind that they were here first!"

"Wait a second, I've got an idea," Maki said. "The ground here is all full of furbit holes. Wouldn't it be terrible if I got my foot caught in one?"

Charlie laughed. "Oh, be careful!" she said. "You might really get stuck!"

Moments later she heard Maki's shouts for help echoing through the forest, followed by the captain grumbling furiously. She scooped Silver up and popped him on her shoulder, then she and Random ducked into the trees.

They stayed low, and as they hurried

past the search party, she heard Maki's
voice. "I did try twisting it!" he yelled.
"Both ways! It's really wedged in!"

Charlie grinned to herself. Maki could
be a pain sometimes, but he deserved
double helpings of pudding for this.

After a while they returned to the trail
and gradually the shouts behind them
faded. The shadows deepened all around
them as the trees grew ever taller.

Silver hopped down and scampered
through the bracken, sniffing and
growling. Then he let out an excited roar,
looking up at Charlie.

"Do you recognise this place?" she
asked. "Are we near your home?"

Silver waved his tail and yowled. Then
suddenly he sprang forward, bounding
over the mossy ground. His silver stripe
flashed as he raced off into the trees.

"Wait!" Charlie shouted after him.

"Silver, wait for us!"

She started running. Random hummed along at her shoulder. Silver darted down a steep hillside covered with boulders and loose shingle. He was making for a dense wall of green vines at the bottom. He glanced back at Charlie, gave another deafening roar, then vanished into the curtain of hanging plants.

Charlie scrambled after him, skidding and sliding to the bottom of the ravine.

"Come on, Random," she said, making for the wall of vines. "His home must be through here!"

She parted the vines and peered through. Great trees rose overhead, blotting out the light. She heard a distant roar, then silence.

She stepped through the vine curtain. Except, somehow, she didn't. She tugged with her foot but something was holding her in place.

She tried to reach down and free her foot, only to find that her arm was caught too. She tugged and struggled but it was held fast by hanging vines clinging to the sleeve of her jacket.

She strained as hard as she could but it only made things worse. As she kicked, the vines got snagged on her trousers, shrinking and tightening like sticky strings.

She felt her feet leave the floor. She was suspended in the air like a fly in a web.

"Random!" she called. "I think I'm stuck."

She tried to turn but her head was caught too. The vines clung to her hair and all around her shoulders.

"Don't worry," the robot said, floating closer with his arms outstretched. "I'm coming, I'll soon have you free."

"Wait," Charlie said. "I'm not sure that's a very good idea!"

But it was too late. Random had taken hold of one of the vines, trying to tug it loose from Charlie's leg. Instead, it stuck to his metal hand, wrapping all the way

around as he tried to pull away.

"How odd," Random said. "I'll just use this hand to – oh."

Now his other hand was stuck too.

"What about your force field?" Charlie suggested. "Can't you use it to protect yourself somehow?"

"I'm trying," Random said, and Charlie heard a loud, annoyed hum emanating from his body. "It seems to have no effect. Perhaps I should try –"

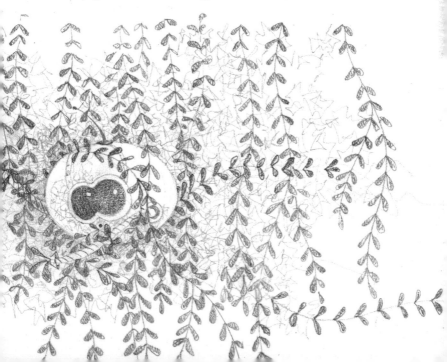

He rolled over in mid-air, trying to twist his arms free. But all that happened was that the vines wrapped themselves completely around his body, tying him up like a birthday present.

Random struggled and buzzed, spinning and tugging. Soon all Charlie could see was a ball of green vines with two angry eyes peering out.

"Well, this is a sticky situation," she said, dangling in place. "How are we going to get loose?"

Chapter Eight
The Clearing

Charlie dangled from the curtain of vines. She felt trapped and annoyed and more than a little silly.

It wasn't uncomfortable. In fact the plants were quite soft, cradling under her arms and around her waist. There was just no way to get free.

She tried to reach her mini-com but it was down in her pocket, and both arms were stuck out at her sides like she was doing star-jumps. Off in the distance she heard a rumble.

"It seems your little friend has abandoned us," Random said, his voice muffled. "And after we brought him all this way!"

"He must be back with his family," Charlie replied. "That's why we came here, after all. I just hope he—"

A deafening roar shook the trees. It was followed by another, and another, a chorus of bellows erupting all around them.

Charlie twisted, trying to look down, or up, or anywhere except straight ahead. It was impossible. She was stuck fast.

She felt something brush against her leg, something furry and ticklish. Something else touched her arm – she could feel it clambering up. In the corner of her eye she could see movement, but she couldn't tell what it was.

There was a gnawing, chomping sound, like someone chewing right next to her ear. Suddenly she found she could move her head. She turned, and found herself looking into a pair of glistening emerald eyes.

"Silver!" she cried out happily. "You came ba—" The vines holding her snapped and she crashed to the ground, landing flat on her back. Looking up, she could see Silver bounding from one vine to the next. For some reason their sticky sap was having no effect on him.

Then she realised that he wasn't alone. There were more rumblebears with him, many more. Most were bigger than Silver, and their fur ranged from deep crimson to fiery brownish-orange. Each had a stripe down its back, but these came in different shades too, from dark grey to pale gold.

The rumblebears swarmed on to the green ball that had once been Random. They clawed and snipped at the vines with

their tiny teeth. There was a creak and the ball dropped, spraying sap as it hit the ground. Random rolled out, eyes spinning.

He activated his force field and rose woozily into the air. Tattered vines clung around his body like a grass skirt. Charlie grinned as the old robot found his balance. "I thought I was going to spend the rest of my days as a green blob."

"Silver saved us," Charlie said proudly. "And his family helped too!"

"These rumblebears are remarkable creatures," Random said. "Their fur must have evolved to be immune to the sticky sap."

"Thank goodness," Charlie said. "Or we could have been up there all day."

Silver nuzzled against her hand. Then he tilted his head towards a line of tall trees. He bounded forward and the rest of his pack followed.

"I think they want us to go with them," Charlie said.

They ducked carefully through the remaining vines, then they climbed a short, mossy slope on the far side. At the top was another line of trees. Sunlight came streaming through the branches.

Charlie felt a swell of excitement as she parted the leaves and pushed through.

She gasped in wonder. Beyond the trees was a huge clearing, almost as large as First Landing itself. It was ringed with giant old trees, with twisted trunks and long, slender branches that shed their coloured leaves on to the grassy ground.

The clearing was pooled with sunlight, and everywhere she looked Charlie could see hundreds of furry rumblebears. They came in all different sizes, from little furballs like Silver right up to large, grey-furred creatures almost as tall as Charlie's knee.

They swung from the branches and rolled around in the sunshine, chattering and roaring as they went. Up in the forked branches and in knotted holes in the trunks she could see soft, comfortable-looking nests, many with tiny, inquisitive infants peering out.

Silver came racing back towards Charlie and she reached down to lift him up. She could feel his heart beating fast beneath her palm.

"So this is your home," she said. "And this must be your pack."

"A pack of thieves," said a voice, and Charlie whipped round.

Captain Robertson stepped between the trees. He was festooned with sticky

vines, dangling from his clothes, his hair and even his moustache. But in his hand was a pair of laser-snips, and on his face was a look of fury.

Chapter Nine
The Picnic

The captain's eyes flashed as he looked out across the clearing. He stared in disgust at the rumblebears as they scampered through the long grass and raced one another up the trunks of tall trees. The vines on his clothes made him look half man and half plant. Charlie would've laughed if he hadn't looked so angry.

Then there was a shout and Maki

bounded between the trees, running up to Charlie. His clothes were free of vines. "The captain stormed in and got stuck!" he said. "The rest of us managed to find a different way round."

Sure enough, their parents soon appeared, followed by the other settlers. Kwame looked amazed as he gazed out across the sun-dappled clearing.

Some of the rumblebears stopped playing and came forward to inspect the newcomers. Maki beamed happily as three of them came bounding up to him. They jumped and scampered and roared deafeningly.

"What an amazing place," Shona said.

"Look at these trees," Kwame agreed. He ran his hand over one of the giant trunks. "They must have grown here for centuries. And it's a good bet the rumblebears have been here just as long."

"Well, they can't stay here any longer."

The captain raised his hand and Charlie saw something dangling from it. It was white and blue, sparkling in the light. A shimmer-apple core.

"These furry fiends have been stealing from us. Here's my proof!"

"But why do you think they've just started stealing our stores now?" Charlie wondered. "There must be a reason for it."

Shona looked

thoughtful, but the captain shook his head. "That's irrelevant," he said. "If we let them remain here, they'll only keep on doing it. They must be driven from my forest before they can cause any more trouble!"

"But where can they go?" Charlie protested. "This glade is their home!"

"I don't care," the captain said briskly. "There must be plenty of places for them to build their little nests. We must find a way to chase them off. Perhaps some kind of sonic device – a loud, constant noise to drive them away."

"No!" Charlie protested. "I've got a better idea."

She reached into her pocket, pulling out a fistful of the hard black fruits she'd found in the pig's trough. She scattered them in the grass and the rumblebears swarmed in, scoffing the rockfruits and letting out a chorus of happy, rattling roars.

"This is their favourite food," Charlie

explained. "Dad says there used to be loads of them down in the valley."

Kwame nodded. "Indeed I did. Until someone made the decision to chop them down." He shot the captain an accusing stare.

"That's the reason they started stealing," Shona realised. "We cut off their food supply."

"So we need to plant more," Charlie said. "Lots more. Then Silver and his friends wouldn't need to steal our food."

"But how long will that take?" the captain demanded irritably. "We can't wait a year for these creatures to start feeding themselves."

Kwame shook his head. "I've got plenty of super-grow powder left. If we sprinkle some around when we plant the trees, we'll get our first crop in a month."

"And until then I suppose we have

to keep feeding them," the captain
grumbled. "From our own precious
stores!"

"I'll eat less," Charlie offered. "And so
will Maki. Won't you?"

Her brother frowned, but eventually he

nodded.

The captain opened his mouth to object, then he looked down in surprise. One of the rumblebears was rubbing against his leg, purring hopefully. The captain looked into the creature's big green eyes, then he let out a sigh.

"Very well," he said. "I suppose they

can stay."

Shona and Kwame grinned and Maki
whooped for joy. Random let out a
bleep of happiness and Silver leapt into
Charlie's arms with a happy roar.

That afternoon they returned to First
Landing and Captain Robertson told
the townsfolk what had been decided.
Many of them were keen to meet their new
neighbours, so Charlie agreed to lead them

up to the rumblebears' glade.

They all brought sacks of food – grain, vegetables and as many rockfruits as they could find on the few trees that were still dotted around the valley. Charlie watched happily as they laid everything out on the grass like a picnic.

Someone took out a fiddle and played an old Earth song. The rumblebears growled and yowled and tried to join in. They raced about the glade, rolling and tumbling. The children of First Landing ran alongside them, laughing and playing.

Silver came racing towards them. His stripe flashed brightly in the evening sunlight. Charlie reached down and he nestled in her arms. She nuzzled his fur, and he let out a roar so loud and sudden that she almost dropped him.

Another rumblebear joined in, and another. Soon the ground beneath their

feet was shaking so hard it felt like a
rocket was about to take off.

The settlers turned to one another
in amazement. Then one by one they
started laughing.

Random bobbed at Charlie's side, a
satisfied look on his metal features.

"Well, I'm very glad it wasn't a terrible beast," he said.

Charlie smiled, hugging Silver close. "I'm not sure the captain would agree with you," she said. "But I love our noisy new friends. It makes me wonder how many other species are out there, just waiting to be discovered!"